MW00978049

To my grandpops and all my other angel friends in heaven.

–CF

To my dear wife , Elizabeth, who with cheerful nature and loving heart, must surely have dwelt with the angels.

–SR

When I Was With The  *Angels*

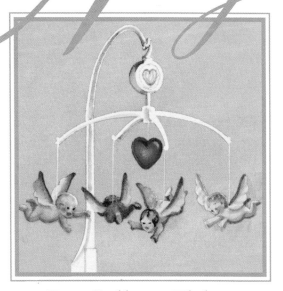

By Colleen Fisher
Illustrated by Stan Rouse

Published by GA Publishing, Inc.
Text copyright © 1996 by Colleen Fisher.
Illustrations copyright © 1999 by Stan Rouse.
All rights reserved. Printed in the U.S.A. No part of this book may be reproduced or copied in any form without written permission from the publisher. All trademarks are the property of
GA Publishing, Inc. Library of Congress Catalog Card Number: 96-94734 ISBN: 0-9652894-7-8

When I was with the angels,
I had FUN!

When I was with
the angels, we'd go
flying over the
mountains. Sometimes
we'd see animals
in the fields below.

When I was with the angels,
we'd play bouncy–bounce
on the clouds–all day long.
We never got tired.

When I was with the angels, we would sit on the stars at night and giggle as they tickled us with their twinkles.

When I was with the angels, we ate all of my favorite foods like tacos, popsicles and cinnamon donuts.

When I was with the angels,
we would sing and dance
and twirl around.
Sometimes I'd get dizzy.

When I was with the angels, we would play
all of my favorite games like
hide–n–seek and ring–around–the–rosy.

When I was with the angels,
I played with my baby sister.
She was there with me, too.

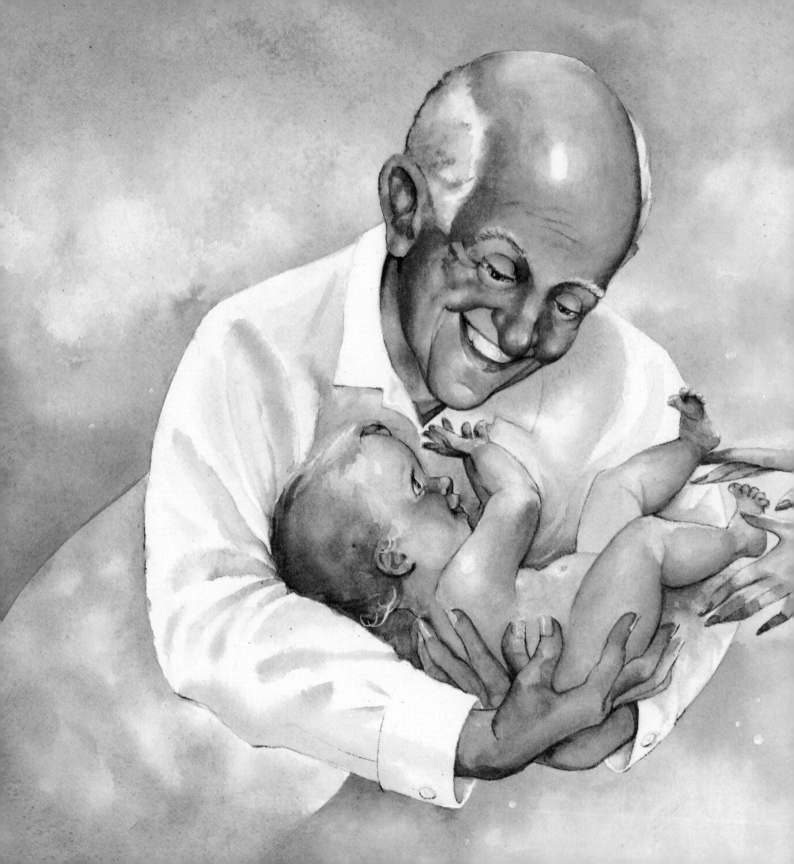

When I was with the angels,
I knew lots of people who had lived before
like my grandpop and my auntie.

BABALLAGOO!

When I was with the angels,
we spoke a silly language
with words like
"baballagoo" and "cakika."

When I was with the angels, I was
with people who loved me a whole lot.
I never wanted to leave.

But one day, the angels told me that
some special people were waiting for me.
These people would also love me
a whole lot.

I was sad to leave the angels.
They were sad, too.
BUT...

I think I'm going
to LOVE
my new home.